A RAINBOW
of Colorful Wishes

MARY ELLEN SHERLOCK
Illustrated by Lynda Farrington Wilson

A RAINBOW of Colorful Wishes

© 2021 Mary Ellen Sherlock
www.maryellensherlock.com

Illustrated by Lynda Farrington Wilson
www.lyndafarringtonwilson.com

ISBN: 978-1-7367809-0-9

To my father, Daniel T. Sherlock
Your stories, Dad, were like a warm
hug...I never wanted them to end. xoxo

Good morning Moms and Dads, Grandmas and Grandpas,
Aunts and Uncles, Cousins and Friends! We are excited
that you are sharing this celebration with us today!
Our Pre-K class is graduating!

I know our boys and girls are so proud of themselves.
They are growing up strong, smart, kind and curious.
Let's give them a round of applause!

We are going to miss you next year but we are
excited for all the really fantastic things you are
going to enjoy in Kindergarten!

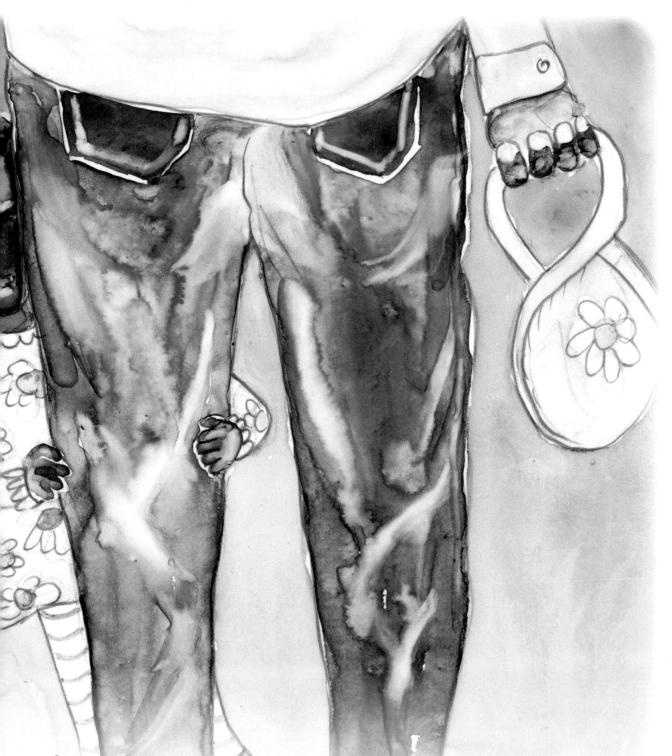

We remember your first days here with us. Some of you were nervous and some were scared. That was OK. You needed to see that school can be fun!

You've learned wonderful things.
You've shared fun memories.
You've made good friends.

We hope you continue to enjoy learning and playing. We are grateful for the time we had to share with you and the chance to watch you grow in brilliant ways. Now, as you leave us, we want to offer you a rainbow of colorful wishes for the incredible future waiting for you.

Our red wish for you is about love. We hope you will be kind to yourself, loving every magical thing that you are. When you love yourself, you will see how easy it is to love other people.

Our orange wish for you is about imagination. All your hopes and dreams can come to life with your imagination. Keep creating, exploring, learning and reading. When you explore different things, you learn even more about who you are.

Our yellow wish for you is about sunlight. Did you know that there is a light inside you? It's true...that light is actually all of your talents and abilities; all the things that make you special. You were born with them. Don't be afraid to share them with the world!

Our green wish for you is about life. We hope you continue to explore, discover and respect all living things...the trees, the flowers, the birds, the animals and the oceans. And even more important, we hope you will do a better job than we did protecting them.

Our blue wish for you is about peace. Everyone of us looks different, talks different, eats different food, likes different things. That's what makes us so awesome! We should celebrate our differences. That's what heroes do! So if you are ever faced with a time when you can choose to be right or you can choose to be kind, we hope you will choose to be kind.

Our purple wish for you is about forgiveness. We hope you will always be brave and have the courage to say three big words... "I am sorry" both to yourself when you need it and others when you've hurt them.

Because my friends, when you forgive, there is peace.
With peace in the world, life grows and grows.
When life grows, the light inside you grows brighter.
Your light makes all your dreams possible.
And we dream of a world filled with endless love.

Congratulations Graduates! We are excited for the colorful future that awaits us as you become the amazing people you were meant to be.

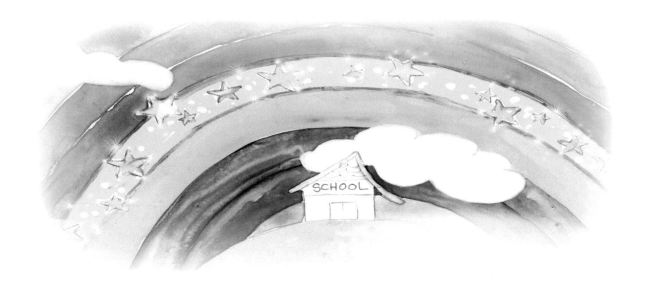

Dedication

Dedicated to Rami, Ribli and the amazing teachers,
staff, families and children of the
Goddard School of Murray Hill, New York

Made in the USA
Monee, IL
22 May 2021